WAITING
OUT
WINTER

Also by Kelli Owen

Teeth
Forgotten
Floaters
The Hatch
Wilted Lilies
Deceiver
Grave Wax
Buried Memories
Survivor's Guilt
Crossroads
Live Specimens
White Picket Prisons
Black Bubbles
The Neighborhood
Waiting Out Winter
Six Days

WAITING
OUT
WINTER

Kelli Owen

Gypsy Press

For Mark and Amanda—thank you for agreeing to leave the winter wonderland.

Acknowledgements: Thanks to Bob Ford and Ron Dickie for pre-reading their little butts off. Thanks to Bob, Brian and Coop for borrowing attitude, verbiage and habits to characters they knew nothing about and are nothing like. And to Paul Goblirsch, for letting a mare play with the stallions of the stable.

Winter either bites with its teeth
or lashes with its tail.

~Proverb

It is not the strongest of the species that survives,
nor the most intelligent. It is the
one that is the most adaptable to change.

~ Charles Darwin

WAITING OUT WINTER

The last of the contaminated died last week, and Nick struggled to accept the parallel truth—the town was free of disease. The parade of unattended funerals was finished, but instead of finding relief, Nick fought the revelation. It felt hopeful, and he had become a pessimist months ago. His logic loomed like a foreboding rain cloud as he reminded himself no one, not even the officials, knew how long the contagion lasted, or if there was such a thing as an immune carrier—and they wouldn't, until another outbreak showed them. Months of paranoia wouldn't simply go away with one death, even if it claimed to be the last.

His dueling reaction continued to battle behind his sleepy eyes. A part of him wanted to walk next door, bang on the boarded windows, and shout to the sky with excitement, relief. But the other part of him knew better than to try to contact neighbors. Everyone had learned last fall that it was safer inside, so most people remained there with their families—or what was left of them—reluctant to trust any evidence, and unwilling to risk going outside if it wasn't absolutely necessary. If there was any celebration of the final death, it was behind locked doors and plastic-covered windows, in small gatherings of survivors.

The Kontis family, like everyone else, had been inside for seven months now—a full five months after the buzzing had stopped. The once innocent sound had become an audible omen, and humanity had tuned in to what it was saying. Through the long winter months, Nick had gradually changed from a night owl to a morning person, and was debating the supposed final death and precursory buzzing while he boiled water for his first morning cup of instant coffee.

As he pulled the hot kettle from the fireplace, before the whistle woke the rest of the family, he heard it. Quiet. Far away. But there nonetheless.

Nick froze. The trembling of his hands caused hot water to slosh inside the dented tin kettle. That damn buzzing.

"No…"

He whispered, as he set the water and coffee cup on the bricks of the fireplace hearth and reached for the flyswatter, which sat collecting dust on the end table. Always within reach, the simple household item had become a tool of survival and there were several in each room of the house. Swatter in hand, Nick stood and attempted to pinpoint the location of the buzzing.

The sound had stopped. He face began to spread in a half smile, not in recognition of humor but in acknowledgement of irony. He mentally compared the situation to elusive noises his truck had teased him with over the years. Whenever he brought it to the shop or got the tools out himself, the noise would mysteriously stop, making it impossible to locate. But the truck's protests of age and abuse were nothing to fear—however, the once harmless yet annoying sound now brought unrivaled terror. He exhaled, trying to convince himself it was his lack of coffee and tired mind playing tricks on him, rather than an actual threat after so many months of anxious safety.

The buzzing resumed and Nick's chest tightened in

response. He looked down the hall where his family slept, unaware of the danger that had entered their shelter. The sound originated in the kitchen, the opposite direction of the bedrooms in the layout of the single-story ranch house. He crept down the hallway, closing doors with a whisper as he went, then turned back the way he'd come. Believing his family was better protected against the intruder, he headed back toward the kitchen. It had been five months since he fought the tiny enemy. He hoped it was like riding a bike.

As he tiptoed into the dark kitchen, the buzzing echoed in the powerless quiet of the house and fear crawled up from his stomach. He remembered the taste of it and thought back to the beginning.

Jerry rolled the windows up and pushed the parental control button to lock them, preventing Scott from lowering them again. "Why do you keep doing that? I'd rather deal with one of Mike's pickled eggs and Old Milwaukee farts." The stench of millions of roadkill worms hung in the air, not necessarily dissipating, but no longer gaining strength through an open window.

"Because I'm a kid at heart?" Scott offered, smirking at Nick before looking out at the black and green highway.

Nick followed Scott's gaze. A thick layer of splattered insects in various stages of decay coated the asphalt. The black areas represented where the soft carcasses had dried, the greenish smears were fresh—or as fresh as death can smell.

"Because we're men," Nick grunted his Tim Allen

impersonation. "Men like foul things."

"Not that foul." Jerry pulled the plastic off another pine-shaped air freshener and waved it around. "I thought they said they were going to do something about this."

The sound of the tent worms popping under their tires reminded Nick of a kid playing with bubble wrap. "Yeah, before we left, they said the DNR was coming in to deal with it."

"Vile things. Sarah's been bitching all summer 'cuz they're eating her cherry tree." Jerry threw the air freshener onto the dash.

"They covered my shed to the point that it looks like my siding is alive—it moves, it's freaky looking." Scott pushed his hand through his thinning hair. "They don't stink as bad when they're alive though." The other two nodded.

"Gas station ahead." Nick pointed between Scott and Jerry's heads from the backseat, having kept watch for the next possible stop. "I need to piss."

"Damn, your bladder gets smaller and smaller with age. You know that?" Jerry glanced at Nick in the rearview mirror.

"Shut it and pull in."

Jerry snickered as he left the county highway for the gravel parking lot. "Now don't take forever, I have a lonely wife to get back to and wonderful things to do to her."

"Damn, man. That's my sister you're talking about—I don't want to hear that!" Nick opened the door as they rolled to a stop and jumped out of the backseat of the quad-cab truck.

In front of the store, an old man regarded him with quiet, ancient eyes as Nick glanced at the battered restroom sign. He pivoted in the gravel toward the side of the building, following the direction of the sign's arrow, and ignored the silent contempt he imagined in the man's stare.

Locating the unisex bathroom, he pushed open the dented metal door and reached for the light switch. Dirty florescence bathed the unwashed room and Nick took in the disgusting ambiance. The dirt-coated floor, smeared from shuffling feet, was an unhealthy color he equated to the stains inside the cracked porcelain of the toilet bowl. Beneath the dirt, the cement floor had been painted the same color as the lower half of the walls—a muddy brown with a random pattern of darker splotches. The color rose up the wall like bile to abut an out of place chair rail, separating it from the filthy, off-white, top-half of the room. Where the stains of rust hadn't grown across it like red algae, the outdated sink, yellowed with age and neglect, perfectly matched the lighter color of the bathroom wall. Nick wondered whether the color combination had been on purpose, and how much of the darker speckles were from design rather than lack of maintenance. He looked up at the weak overhead light, wondering if a colored bug-bulb gave the bathroom its ironic excremental hues. Instead, he saw several dozen fly-strips hanging from the ceiling around the uncovered white florescent tube.

"Damn," he grimaced at the black bodies covering the sticky amber strips by the hundreds. "Clean the bathroom and maybe you wouldn't have this problem." Nick wished his journalistic mind didn't always have to absorb every detail and quickly used the facilities without touching anything beyond the doorknob.

Out front again, he waved at the guys in the truck and motioned he was grabbing a drink from inside, Jerry waved the pine tree air freshener at him and Nick acknowledged the request with a thumbs up.

As Nick approached the door, he noticed the old man's arms were covered in open wounds, oozing an infectious combination of blood and pus. The man wore stained, torn pants, and an equally dirty tank top that was all but thread-bare and appeared to have become one with the man's skin in a few places. The signature flannel shirt wasn't missing, Nick noted, but wadded up in the man's lap, wet from sweat or pus, or a combination of the two. The man absently scratched at his arm as he looked up at Nick, one eye swollen shut by a bruise, which may have started as a wound similar to those on his arms but had definitely progressed into another abscess.

"They knew. They knew it would happen." The man wiped an infection-smeared hand across his face and swatted at something in the air. "Weren't no accident. Don't care. Never cared. Did it on purpose. Can't find Sam-Dog either. Probably a Greener now. You seen Sam-Dog?"

The old man sneered at Nick and waited for a response. His lip curled and showed off a checkerboard smile—dark recesses of missing teeth were neighbored by unhealthy, tobacco-stained nubs that hung precariously, waiting to fall away from the inflamed gums, which fought to support them. "No matter. You see him, you do what's right and put him down. You're not one of them. No suit. No safety. Hey, where's your hat, boy?"

Nick opened his mouth to speak but decided against it. Other than Jerry's truck, the parking lot held an older pickup truck, a dirty but newer model blue Taurus, and a classic Schwinn bicycle held together by duct tape—a canvas bag hanging off the bent handlebars. He decided the bike fit the baffling curmudgeon best and pushed the door open to distance himself from the obviously sick man.

Inside it was cooler and Nick was impressed the little roadside station would have air conditioning. His momentary respect for the place quickly dissolved when he noticed the windows were nailed shut and fly-strips were hung like forgotten Christmas decorations. He looked across the top of the low shelving units, located the soda, and walked to the back cooler to grab three Cokes. A reflection in the door caught his attention as the glass swung shut again.

Nick turned toward the woman and child in the next aisle, his brows gathering in confusion. What planet had he and the boys driven in to? It was easily eighty degrees outside and this woman had her child bundled up like it was the middle of winter. The poor kid had to be sweating underneath the full snowsuit, mittens and ski mask. Sure, it was air conditioned in here, but it wasn't cold.

A glance up at the mother merely provided further confusion. He guessed the woman was somewhere in her late twenties, but she could easily pass as a decade or better older by the haggard features and washed, worn expression. She kept one hand on the faded purple of her daughter's snowsuit shoulder at all times and constantly scanned the area around her through squinted, discerning lids, as if scoping the joint out in order to snatch expired products from the shelf in a senseless victory against the system. But something in her eyes reminded Nick of fear. Not the fear of being caught or fear of a missed opportunity. Something deeper echoed from the bag-lined blues and heavy sleep-deprived lids. She swatted at the air randomly, further adding to the mystique of the strange inhabitants of the sideshow gas station. Nick shook his head and filed it away, wishing he had brought his camera with him. It wasn't Pulitzer material, but he was fairly certain any one of the reporters at work could have come up with a decent human-interest story to go along with the photo. He paid for the sodas and headed back to the truck, forgetting about the air freshener.

As the door swung behind him, he heard the old man muttering in the chair outside, "Shame we're out of strips and swatters. Maybe some will come in next week." Nick paused and thought about asking the old man what the hell he was talking about, but blew it off as senility.

"What took you so long?" Jerry started the engine and popped the truck into drive, rolling forward before Nick's ass even hit the seat. "Christ the stink is going to kill us out here."

"The stink?" Nick pulled his door shut. "Oh, the tent worms. I forgot all about them in the Twilight Zone Gas Station. It must not stink as bad here as it did on the highway."

"Twilight Zone?"

"Yeah." Nick told them about the mother and child, sick old man, and fly-strip factory of a bathroom.

"Didn't notice the pumps, did ya?" Scott nodded as they drove past and Nick saw the weathered sign on the front of the old fashion gas pump, "Out of Gas--Delivery Soon." But "Soon" had been crossed through with a marker and the word "Never" had been scrawled underneath it. "No biggie, we have enough gas to get home. New truck has dual tanks..."

"Yeah, but it's still a weird little gas station." Jerry spoke as he hit the pavement and gunned it out of there. "Maybe I'll stop picking on all of Sarah's bad horror movie choices for having freaky gas stations—apparently, it's based in reality." They laughed uncomfortably.

The next two hours were quiet, except for the popping of tent worms under speeding tires. Two more gas stations without gas and only one other vehicle on the road had made all three men glance at each other with raised eyebrows and unspoken questions. Nick noticed fly-strips hanging in clusters from every house they passed along the desolate stretch of the small less-traveled county road. Maybe they'd always been there. Maybe he was just noticing them because of the gas station bathroom. But something in the pit of his stomach rolled over.

"Turn the radio on." Nick's request broke the silence and startled Jerry. Scott remained slouched against the window and Nick presumed his life-long friend had fallen asleep in the quiet truck.

"Sure. Am I taking requests?"

"See if you can find any news."

"News? Your vacation isn't over until Monday morning. You have a whole 'nother day to relax."

"Just humor me." Nick was mildly annoyed Scott had not given up shotgun before he took a nap. The roadtrip rule had been practiced for over a decade, and if he were in front, Nick would be able to flip stations without voicing his desire for news rather than music. He could have avoided Jerry's ribbing, and wanted to punish Scott by shaking his seat to wake him, but he let it slide.

The crackling and hissing from the radio came on louder than expected and Jerry turned the volume down before hitting scan to get off his preset stations. They weren't close enough to home for any of those to come in clearly and he would have to search for the nearest one. Broken static occasionally interrupted the quiet of the speakers as the tuner searched fruitlessly. Nick met

Jerry's eyes in the review mirror and understood instantly that neither of them was sure whether it was out-of-range stations or hiccups in the towers causing the off-air sounds. Jerry pressed the button and resumed scanning. The digital numbers went through their full range twice but produced nothing. None of the popping and crackling of weak stations were even strong enough to pause the search mode. Jerry glanced back at Nick. "I've got a few CDs in the glove box."

"Nah, I really was looking for news."

"Why?"

"Nothing. Over-active imagination."

Outside his window, past the green and black smear the bug-slathered highway had become, Nick watched the wildlife, or rather, lack thereof. He noted the crows that should have dotted the shoulder, eating whatever they could find on the pavement—road kill or even the grisly remains of millions of tent worms—were absent. He was debating the possibility of the stench being too much for even the decay-eating scavengers and vermin of the area, when he spotted a coyote wandering along the opposite side of the road ahead of them. Nick blamed the visible limp for the predator's strange canter. As they neared the wild dog, he saw the normal onset of winter mange was much worse than it should have been. Crusted mud in the animal's fur pulled clumps of matted hair in every direction and gave the illusion of bald patches.

While there was a noticeable lack of living wildlife amongst the overabundance of worms, regular roadkill—raccoon, skunk and deer—still punctuated the highway. There seemed to be a lot of them, but there always were this time of year, so Nick blew it off and studied the worm-ruined bare trees instead. The foliage was all but gone.

When they'd left for their trip, two weeks beforehand, it had looked like only certain trees were going to suffer under the onslaught of tent worms. Now, however, the truth settled in, as Nick noticed the only trees untouched by the vile caterpillars was the evergreens. Apparently the little bastards preferred leaves to needles.

The last time he'd seen the worms swarm had been back in high school, but it wasn't as bad as this year. He remembered them saying there was a cycle for the insects. He didn't remember the exact number they'd said back then but guessed this year was peak season again—and then some. He also didn't remember the smell. Maybe it was worse this year, or maybe it was just one of those memories you don't preserve. As a teen, he'd found sick humor in the whole thing, and they'd tossed the bugs into bonfires by the shovelful that summer. As an adult, he still had a sick sense of humor, but the destructive nature of the creatures affected him more, perhaps because he had more to lose—it was his trees, his lawn, and his tax dollars fighting them. Either way, the worms were back and doing a bang-up job of imitating a biblical locust raid.

He leaned back and closed his eyes, intending to relax rather than sleep, "How much longer?"

"A few hours or so. Depends on traffic." Jerry snickered at his own joke regarding the abnormal lack of vehicles. Nick smiled for Jerry's benefit and let his mind wander behind closed lids. "So at least an hour before we're out of the deadzone?"

"At least. Fucking hills block towers up here even when you're right next to them."

"Yeah. It doesn't help that we don't have a national company. The little local boys suck for reception." Nick listened to the popping of the worms. "Why don't you throw a CD in just for some noise?"

"You got it." Jerry reached over and pulled a blue CD from the glove box. Nick was unconscious before the first song started.

At the outskirts of town they tried the radio again, knowing exactly which channels should work. None did. Static greeted them from the speakers, screaming volumes of silence their echoed glances told Nick he had unnerved them both.

As they rolled into what should have been a busy weekend downtown, they found the streets empty. School was out, but no kids were anywhere to be seen. Half the cars that should have been parked on the streets were missing.

While Nick's leg began to bounce in nervous habit, he noticed the streetlights were set to flashing--yellow one direction, red the other. The A&W and Dairy Queen both had their "Closed for the Season" signs hung and front windows boarded—and it was only the beginning of September. Several dogs and a cat wandered around, their collars marking them as pets rather than feral. Yet, they seemed mangy, wild, and limped with a similarity that made them tame versions of the coyote he'd seen earlier.

Jerry slapped Scott's leg, jostling him from sleep, and pointed to the empty beachfront. They raised eyebrows at each other and Scott turned toward Nick. Nick nodded and allowed his thoughts to roll freely. The town was too quiet. Something had happened. Jerry tried the radio again, while Scott shifted uncomfortably in his seat as they passed the closed grocery store and unoccupied playgrounds. Nick flipped his phone open and hit the speed dial for home. It disconnected immediately with a popup on his screen that declared "network busy." Scott tried his phone and judging from the look he gave him, Nick assumed Scott had gotten the same message.

Jerry didn't bother with his phone. "Did we go to war?"

There it was. The question Nick figured they were all wondering, given power by being uttered by someone other than him.

"We'd know, wouldn't we?" Scott tried denial. It was odd for Nick to see the accountant act that way. Scott was a straight facts kind of guy, always construing from the given to come up with the logical conclusion. Obviously, something had happened, but not even Scott was going to voice which of the several horrible possibilities it could be.

Unlike Nick, Jerry had no imagination. Unlike Scott, he didn't deduce from fact. Jerry worked off gut instinct, and his gut usually worked through his mouth. "Well what else could it be?" He fumbled in the backpack on the seat between Scott and himself, and pulled out his chew. "Damn Middle East has been just waiting to explode for how long?" He flicked his wrist several times, tobacco audibly slapping the inside of the tin.

"No, we definitely would have heard about it. Something. Mike would have managed a call from whatever hellhole he's in this week and let us know." Scott argued, trying to negate the horrendous possibility.

"How? Our cell phones had no range in the woods. We couldn't even call home the last few weeks, let alone the damn Middle East." Nick interjected and Jerry shot him a glare in the review mirror, making him wish he'd have let them argue through it on their own.

"Well then, at the gas stations or something." Scott turned to Nick.

"But we didn't ask either. Maybe they assumed we knew?" Nick shrugged.

"Not war. Doesn't seem right." Jerry recanted his conclusion as he shoved a thick pinch of raw tobacco into his mouth and used his tongue to wedge it between his lip and gum. "Something happening somewhere else wouldn't get kids off the street. Wouldn't leave pets wandering..."

"True. Maybe we should just get home and find out."

"Ok. You first, Nick?"

"Sure, I'm closest." He chewed his lip, trying to figure out what could have possibly cleared the streets.

They pulled up in front of Nick's house at the west edge of town. His street looked like the rest of Hayward had: vehicles were missing and several windows were covered with what appeared to be plastic.

"Early winter storm?" Through the side window, he checked his neighborhood and then up towards the sky.

"Sky doesn't look rainy, let alone snowy." Jerry spit tobacco juice into the empty Coke bottle in his hands. "And storms are broadcast on all the channels, but there's only dead air."

"Let's just get home and recoup, figure out what the hell is up." Jerry didn't look at Nick, not even via the rearview mirror. He stared forward at the empty street in front of him.

Nick grabbed his bags from the back of the pickup and told them to call him when they got home. They nodded and drove away.

"Shut the door!" Jamie ran toward Nick from the

kitchen. He dodged his wife as she slammed the door shut and patted down the duct tape that had been put up all around it. "You'll let them in, for God's sake! What are you thinking?"

"Jamie..." He stopped, her expression melted from panic to relief. She wrapped her arms around his neck and fell against him.

"Oh, thank God you're home." She lifted her hand and he thought she was going to slap him for a moment. Instead, she felt his forehead. "No fever? Any signs of sickness? Are you guys all ok? We've been so worried..." Her questions ran together, her speech sped up like an anxious teenager.

"Daddy!" Nick saw the boys behind Jamie and knelt down in time to catch Hunter and Tyler as they launched themselves at him. He squeezed them together in a group hug and then pulled back to look in their faces.

"Mommy says I can go hunting with you in a few years."

"Yes, you can. When you're twelve, Hunter."

"What about me?"

"When you're twelve."

"But twelve is forever. Will we be able to go outside again when I'm twelve?"

Nick looked up at Jamie, unsure how to answer a question he didn't understand and waiting for her to explain. Instead she pulled the boys from Nick and shooed them back toward the kitchen.

"You can play with daddy and plan your trips in a bit. Right now I need to talk to him."

"But ma..."

"No." She spoke sternly but through a smile that was classic Jamie and made Nick feel better about the strange circumstances. "Now go finish your snacks and color for a while. Tall talk."

Tyler kicked at the carpet and turned away. Hunter squeezed his father again and left the room without looking at his mother. Nick smiled at the boys but the grin was meant for Jamie and her stolen Jurassic Park line they'd adopted years beforehand.

"Jamie?" For the first time since walking in the door, Nick looked around the room. He didn't recognize his own home. He noted the plastic, duct tape and mismatched cardboard from boxes and soda packs covering all the windows. Vents were blocked. Furniture was rearranged. And fly-strips hung like tinsel from everything that would hold a tack. Some were old and covered in dust and dead black bodies. Others were fresh, shining with new glue.

He and the guys had spent two years coordinating the two-week hunting trip. The wives were fine with it, as they'd always done weekend trips ice fishing or camping over the years. They'd almost cancelled when Mike's unit was called back to the Middle East, but the trip had turned into a need rather than want when Scott's divorce got ugly and ended with his ex-wife moving two states away with his children, but calling him almost every day to continue to complain about this, that and the other thing. Scott needed to get away from everything and everyone, and the remaining three decided to go with Mike. The trip had included more campfire and beer than it had hunting, but had been rejuvenating. The house around him, though—combined with Jamie's behavior and Tyler's question—made him think he'd returned to an alternate universe.

"What the hell is going on? Other than the hospital parking lot, it looks like the whole damn town has gone into hiding or been evacuated."

"They have. It has. Stop joking around." She backed up and stared at him a moment. "You haven't heard? You're not... You're not joking..."

"Jamie—"

"The flies. Well, I suppose it was really the tent worms."

"The worms?"

"No, the DNR and their fucking brilliant ideas. That's what it was." Anger sharpened her voice as she rambled at him.

"What? Slow down." He led her to the couch and eased her down, watching her face the entire time. "What happened? From the beginning."

"People are dying. Dying from the flies."

"Hon," he waited for her to make direct eye contact. "The beginning..."

She inhaled and looked toward the kitchen for a moment. "Ok."

"The boys?"

"They're fine." Her eyes danced across his face and fell to the carpet. "Right before you left, remember the DNR saying they were going to take care of the worms?"

"Damn tent worms are still all over the highway. It stunk like hell in the thicker parts—you'd think it was dinosaur roadkill from the stench."

"Yeah, well, their bright idea was to release black biting flies. By the droves. Because they supposedly eat tent worm larvae and would therefore eat the problem before their peak cycle became a problem."

"Really? That was their great idea?"

"Well they fucked up." She looked up at him, anger brimming behind her eyes as she ignored his interjection.

"They released them too late and the larvae had already hatched. The flies don't eat the worms, only the eggs and babies, so we're stuck with the worms."

"Ok, that explains why they're still all over and systematically eating the forest. Have you seen that? It's unbelievable the damage they're doing."

"You're not listening." She put her hand on his shoulder and squeezed. "They screwed up. The DNR. So we were stuck with the tent worms, and then we were swarmed with black biting flies."

"Ah, ok. That explains the fly-strips everywhere."

"But we got a double-whammy." Her fingernails bit into his shoulder. "The flies were, well... Infected, I guess you'd call it."

"Infected with what?"

"There's the million dollar question." Jamie raised her voice again. She sat back and glanced again at the kitchen before returning in a hushed tone. "First they said cholera, then anthrax, and finally they admitted it didn't have a name but was similar to a strain of bubonic plague that had been all but wiped out." Her speech sped up again near the end of the sentence as she tried to get it all out in one breath. He couldn't tell if it was anger or impatience.

"They said it wouldn't be a problem. That it was only infectious to animals. Did you notice Buddy wasn't barking? That's because Buddy died. But not before his fur fell out and his eyes became bulges of bloodshot sickness and he became more vicious than he's ever pretended to be."

Nick realized he had been so confused with the state of the town he hadn't noticed the next-door neighbor's wolfhound hadn't threatened to tear him to shreds for being in his own yard. He hated that dog. He'd hated that dog since the day it decided to hate everyone, friend and foe. It barked at the mailman, the children playing outside, hell, even the wind. It had gone from being a neighbor's dog he didn't give a crap about, to an animal he couldn't stand the sight of. Making matters worse, the Browns never bothered to tell Buddy to stop or bring him inside when he continued. Nick disliked them for their lack of action far more than he hated the dog. The dog was an annoyance, the neighbor was a nuisance, and the difference was astronomical in Nick's mind. For all his barking, Buddy would have never bitten anyone. He was one of those dogs who pretended to be mean—growling and snarling to put on a good show—but if you pet him you became his friend for the day—although he'd start the attitude all over the next time he saw you. Once upon a time they'd joked that if a burglar could get past the façade and pet him, Buddy would show them where the valuables were.

"Died?"

"Yeah. But they lied and people started getting sick. So they said stop eating meat—claiming it came from sick cattle—but people were still getting sick. Then they said they had a chemical that would kill it and quarantined everyone inside for three days while they dusted the tri-county area—thank God you guys were further south!

"But that didn't work either. And now people won't go outside. The government is starting to track the movements south and is saying the flies are going to spread to the entire North American continent within a few months. And only when they were forced by some government committee did they even acknowledge or admit they'd given the flies the disease on purpose."

"On purpose?"

"Yeah. They were working on developing something that would kill off birds and take care of the Avian Flu, and they let those flies loose instead of regular black biting flies. Those flies! The flies they infected with something that was only supposed to kill animals but had never left the lab before. Had never been tested. The bastards—"

Nick cut her off, seeing her anger boil to a point that would draw the attention of the boys in the other room. "So the flies are diseased? And they won't eat the worms, but they'll kill us? Is that really what you're saying?" His incredulous expression hardened as the repercussions began to solidify in his mind.

"Yes."

He reached for the T.V. remote and she stopped him, putting her hand over his. "Don't bother."

"Since when?"

"It seemed like the moment you walked out the door, but I guess it's only been a week since the televisions and radios went silent. No one wanted to even go out for their mail or to walk their dogs, let alone go to work—so there's no one to man the stations. For a few days we had national broadcasts, they must have set them like that before they abandoned the stations, but those are gone now, too."

"That explains the stray pets downtown."

"Yeah, they left the neighborhoods after ransacking all the garbage cans. I suppose they're digging in the business dumpsters now."

"So what are we doing? When will they have it dealt with?"

"We don't know." Her sentence hung in the air like it was waiting for clarification, but none came.

Nick looked at her and realized she was wearing full length pants, socks and a long sleeve t-shirt. If Jamie was anything, it was a tank top and shorts kind of girl. She always had been, even in the dead of winter, so long as she was in the house. Seeing her in this much clothing in late summer or early fall was unusual at best, unnerving at worst. Could the problem really be as bad as she claimed?

The phone rang and broke the silence.

"Let the machine get it, I'm sick of the gossipers spreading fear and asking the same three questions every day."

"What if it's the guys? They were going to call when they got home."

She shrugged and he walked over to the small table that held the phone, an empty flower vase—unusual as well, as Jamie picked fresh flowers for it almost daily as long as they continued to grow—and a green porcelain dish with a pewter squirrel on it his grandmother had given them which they used for loose change and car keys. The caller I.D. showed Sarah and Jerry's phone number and he picked it up.

"Hell—"

"Oh Nick! I'm so glad you're home. Mom's been calling every day and none of the authorities were willing to send anyone to locate you and—"

"Sarah, breathe, hon. I'm home, Jerry's home, everyone is safe. Let me talk to Jerry for a second, okay?"

Rather than an answer from his sister, Jerry's voice responded. "You believe this shit?"

"I don't know. I just got the basics and it's still sinking in."

"I got the high-speed cliff notes. Never knew your

sister could talk like that." Nick heard Jerry spit and imagined the paper cup Sarah demanded he use in the house. "The worms then the flies, then the pets and kids and elderly... Damn, Nick, what the hell are we going to do?"

"Kids and elderly?" He spoke into the phone but questioned Jamie with his eyes. She nodded and turned away from him.

"Let me call you back, okay? Call around and see what you can find out. We need the full story here and communications being cut off will make that difficult. Is Wade still working for the county or did he transfer already?"

"Nah, he's there until December, then he goes south for small town sheriff duty."

"Call him."

"Will do."

Neither man said good-bye, simply hung up. Nick turned back to his wife and saw her shoulders slumped. He could hear her breathing and knew she was upset, but didn't think she was crying. Yet.

"Jamie, what about the kids and elderly? Our parents? Emily?"

Without turning around or looking up she answered in a broken voice. "They're fine. I mean parents and Emily. I'll never understand you and Sarah. You love each other to death but have barely spoken since she married Jerry—yet you take him everywhere with you. Whatever... the elderly and kids though... dead, dying, infected. I was trying to tell you."

Nick knelt in front of her. He grabbed her hands and leaned down, willing her to make eye contact. "I'm listening. Tell me everything."

"Everything" included slowly revealed details, some of which were difficult for Jamie to share and almost as hard for Nick to hear. When the disease spread to humans it attacked the weakest first, the elderly and children. Children played outside, unconcerned with tent worms and only annoyed by the flies, and therein became easy pickings for the flying beasts with infectious scissor-like teeth. The elderly may have spent more time indoors, but they were more susceptible due to immune system deficiencies. The first case was actually thought to be bedsores, until they spread, rapidly covering the poor woman and hospitalizing her within forty-eight hours. Her fever rose to 104 and the tiny blisters popped, leaking into any and all wounds, scratches or other abrasions in her thin, aging skin. She was dead within ten hours and panic slowly started to rumble through the hospital, then it reverberated through the town around it.

Those that knew reacted as quietly as they could, pulling their children from daycare, calling in sick, stocking up on food and supplies. But as is the nature in small towns, gossip travels quickly, and when it is not fed directly, it's imagined by the actions of others. Suggestion leads to supposed truths, which leads to new rumors based on absolutely nothing concrete. By the end of the first week, there were six dead and several dozen sick, but the word on the street was much higher numbers.

Nick learned almost everyone had firsthand experience with the infection, through a family member, coworker or neighbor and stared with his mouth agape as Jamie told him the horrors of their own neighborhood.

"Terry was the first and that poor girl of his found him." The divorced dad across the street had been nothing short of the perfect father to his eleven-year-old daughter, and Nick frowned as concern for the girl welled inside him. "Last I heard, she was staying with her grandmother while they tried to figure out if they could even locate the mother. I don't know if they ever did.

"It happened so quickly. From release to enough deaths to cause panic was only five days. People had begun dropping like, well... flies."

The irony of the lifespan of the infected being drastically shorter than that of the insect biting them was not lost on Nick. "Will the disease die when the flies die?"

"No. It's part of them. It'll reproduce with them. Genetically altered and all that shit."

Nick wasn't sure he could believe something that hadn't come to fruition yet and wanted to ask if this was her opinion or official word from the government, but he remained quiet and allowed Jamie to spew forth all the ugliness he'd missed, hoping it would cleanse her of it in some way.

Jamie explained how, after the tenth death, everyone swarmed the grocery stores for food, hardware stores for supplies, and ran their credit cards up as they wore their checkbooks down—often overdrawing them in the name of survival.

"But where is everyone? I mean, why not stockpile supplies in one place? Make a stand as a group?"

"We were, initially... well, sort of. Groups formed in churches and schools and businesses, but that all fell apart when people realized no one could trust who was or wasn't sick. In the interest of self-preservation, everyone has turned their backs on everyone else. Hell, I dare you to try and knock on a door! They all shut the world out. Some ran off to relatives and cabins in other parts of the country—afraid the government would burn Hayward to the ground with napalm or something. Kill off the disease and count us as collateral damage."

"It's not impossible, but I think far too many people believe it's as common a solution as Hollywood would like us to believe." He quickly counted off the movies he could recall that had used the technique, whether in the United States or elsewhere to deal with anything from disease to alien invasion. "And if anything, it would be precise strikes, not grand sweeping genocide. Most likely the woods—"

Jamie continued as if he hadn't spoken. "Telephones and television and radio helped those of us that stayed behind. But everything changed when the static began."

"When was that?"

"Wednesday? Nine days or so after the initial fly dump."

"Unmanned stations?"

"Well, there were a few theories. I preferred that one, but Sarah heard it was because it was worse out there—that everyone else was dead. Rebecca told us it was because they'd just turned off our feed so we couldn't see how bad it was, and that made sense in a weird way. After all, why aren't our national stations and cable and satellite and such working? Cartoon Network doesn't come out of Duluth or Eau Claire, it comes out of California or something doesn't it? Damn media tells us too much when we don't want to know and not enough when we need to know."

"You're right. I like the first option best. Phones?"

"All still working—landlines and cell." She looked up and Nick realized the boys were standing in the doorway of the kitchen listening. She lowered her voice to finish her thought, "But how long will telephone and electricity last with no one doing maintenance downtown and none of us working to pay our bills?"

He turned and motioned the boys to come on out. Nick squeezed his children, relieved they hadn't been part of the horror stories Jamie had told him. As he rolled on the floor with them, he outwardly shared their innocent enthusiasm and reckless abandon. Inside, his mind churned with dark thoughts and apocalyptic possibilities, and took note of their total coverage wardrobe.

Nick thought about the information overload Jamie had dumped on him and came to the conclusion that what had initially been a controlled situation had turned into a contained paranoia. He was glad to be home, but it wasn't the home he'd left behind. It was darker, physically and mentally. A nightmare he had no control over.

By nightfall, he had heard back from Jerry. Wade had provided no new information in a huff that let Jerry and Nick know, even in his official position, Wade was being left out of the loop and wasn't happy about it. Nick tried to accept the situation while watching his family dine on vegetarian lasagna—Jamie had refused to get fresh meat and was saving their frozen pre-infection stores for future use, thanking him for his hunting hobby and two freezers worth of venison, bear and fish. After dinner, he began formulating a plan for survival.

Believing they had added strength in numbers, regardless of the town's failure at the same notion, they moved his sister Sarah's family into the Kontis' larger home. Shuffling bedrooms and rearranging Nick's home office and the kids' playroom in the basement, they easily made it roomy enough for the addition of Jerry, Sarah and little Emily. Sarah spent most of her time with Emily or talking quietly to Jamie. Nick hated their new relationship and wished he could figure out how to fix it. But he knew he'd pushed her too far the night before her wedding and she'd never forgive him for his words. It wasn't that Jerry was a bad guy—Nick just thought he was wrong for his sister and had told her as much. Now, with the situation and sudden closeness of Sarah and Jerry, he wished he could take those words—hell, the whole night—back.

They were still settling in when they offered to let Scott join them, but he chose to drive to Indiana to be near his children, "The ex's opinions be damned." He claimed it wasn't the fear of government solutions but a desire to protect his children, and he left as the rumors of the Illinois and Indiana borders being breeched by the flies hit the Hayward rumor mill. Nick and Jerry knew Scott well enough to know there was at least a touch of government paranoia behind his hurried exit, but they let their friend go without voicing it. Mike called from a three-day leave in Turkey to check on them. He wouldn't be home anytime soon and only knew there was massive troop recall for support and the National Guard had been called to arms. Mike was surprised the Army would send troops from other states to his own. Nick's imagination wondered if the Army believed it was easier to quarantine, and kill if necessary, your own countrymen as long as they weren't your own neighbors and family members. He kept that thought to himself as well, concentrating instead on keeping everyone's spirits up.

Jerry and Nick made several trips covered in industrial strength repellant that permanently burned flesh where their skin was exposed at the edges of their clothing. While they were out, the women busied themselves rearranging the house to keep necessities at hand and put away those things that were no longer needed for every day life. They all tried to make life as normal as possible for the kids.

Normal meant lying for the most part. Playing videos so the kids didn't ask questions about why the television didn't work. Removing the radios from sight so Hunter and Tyler wouldn't request they be turned on. Even snagging playroom equipment and games while out for real supplies was done in the name of making things look and feel normal. Nick knew it wouldn't last, but he didn't know how much the children comprehended until he stumbled upon them coloring.

"No they don't."

"Yes. Mom said." Tyler, the younger of the two, sniffled as his brother argued with him.

"Well if it worked then we'd be outside and we're not, so just shut up."

"Hey, hey. We don't talk like that, Hunter." Nick squatted down to talk to the boys, careful not to block the television and it's fiftieth airing of Toy Story. "What's going on here?"

"Nothing." Hunter stabbed at his paper with the dark crayon and added to the marks already scattered about the page.

"Well, if there's a problem you know you can come to us if you can't work it out."

"Won't do any good." Hunter traded the dark crayon for a brick red.

"Hunter?" Nick studied the drawing his son was working on for a few moments. It looked like a giant Popsicle dripping blood and concern knit Nick's brows together. "So, what are you drawing?"

"Stupid flies."

"Ahhh…" The Popsicle was in fact a crude flyswatter. "So these are the flies?" Nick pointed to the black dots.

"No, these are." Hunters finger circled the collection of red speckles between the swatter and the black spots. "Those are the dead people."

Nick swallowed and looked at Tyler. The boy had stopped coloring and pulled his legs up tight to his chest. His eyes welled with tears and Nick felt the lump form in his throat. "Is this what you guys were arguing about?"

"Yes."

"No." Hunter crumbled his drawing and threw it at his younger brother.

"Hunter…"

"Will we ever be able to go outside again?" Tyler interrupted, a tear run down his cheek and his fear caused his voice to tremble. "Mommy says we will. She says the flies will die."

"They will. Or at least they'll hibernate."

Nick knew Tyler understood the word from all the hunting shows he'd watched with the boys, but clarified for the confused expression his younger son's snarled lip projected. "They'll go to sleep when it gets cold."

"But it's already cold and we're still stuck in here. I don't want to be in here any more!" Hunter jumped up and ran to the front door. Nick stood and moved to stop him but Sarah intercepted him.

"Honey… what's going on?" She grabbed Hunter and pulled him to her as she gave her brother a questioning nod.

"I don't want to die!" Tyler wailed and ran down the hall toward the bedrooms.

"Go… get Tyler. I've got Hunter." Sarah picked up the eight-year-old with a grunt and headed toward the kitchen doorway where Jamie stood.

"Nick," Jamie's voice stopped him and he turned

around. "I'll get Tyler. Scott's on the phone. He's at Cheryl's… Sounds upset, you better take it." They traded duties as she handed him the phone before heading down the hallway.

Nick shut his eyes and exhaled, "Hey Scottie, what's up?" Silence answered him and he pulled the phone away from his ear to look at it, as if it were a cell phone and he'd know if the connection was lost. He put it back to his hear and listened for a moment. He could barely make out the ragged breathing on the other end.

"Scott?" He nudged with a soothing tone. Scott had never been a quiet person, they'd teased him all through college about never shutting up, and Nick immediately worried if Scott or the kids had been bitten. "Hey, man—"

"Cheryl's dead." Scott's voice was calm but trembling, cracked.

"Dead? When? When did you get there?" Nick retreated to the kitchen and let Jamie and Sarah handle the boys on their own. Jerry sat at the table, eyebrows raised at Nick's questions. Nick covered the phone and told Jerry, "Cheryl's dead." Jerry covered his mouth with his hand and shook his head before spitting tobacco juice into the Dixie cup he held.

Scott continued on the phone, "I just got here… half hour ago maybe, or an hour, I don't know." Scott's steady voice of logic cracked as he spoke. "Randy said she died last night. And Nick… he's coughing."

"Oh shit, Scott. I'm sorry." Jerry's looked up at Nick's word choice and Nick waved him off. "Is there any chance it's just a cold?"

"No. He was bit. He knows it and he knows what it means. He's actually being quite brave for eight."

Nick thought of his Hunter and how very different his behavior was from Scott's boy. "What about Michelle?"

"She's fine, but she's in shock. Randy said Cheryl coughed pretty hard at the end. Michelle was sitting with her and got covered in blood. She hasn't spoken since… she was still speckled in blood when I got here…" The ragged breathing turned to sobs and Nick waited for Scott to regain his composure and finish his thought.

Silence answered him.

"Scott? What do you want to do? What are you going to do?"

"I don't know. I don't fucking know." His voice skipped. "I mean… I still loved her. And her kids needed her. But I can't fix it or change it… and now Randy…"

"Come back here." Nick was startled by his tone. He had meant it as a suggestion but it had sounded more like a demand. "You know, you could come here. Hole up with us instead of down there by yourself."

"I don't know. I can't do anything… I can't even think straight. Randy—"

"It's ok. Just calm down. Maybe it's not fatal for everyone." Nick glanced at Jerry, their eyes acknowledged the lie he'd just uttered.

"I can't… I… I'll call you later."

The phone went dead.

"Shit." Nick set the phone on the table.

"Cheryl and Randy?"

"Yeah. Damn." Nick pulled out the chair next to Jerry and sat. "Maybe we should drive there and get him."

"What? How?" Jerry stood and paced the small room as Nick's leg began bouncing with nervous energy. "We can't. We can't risk contaminating everyone all the way down and then back and then bring it into this house. We made it safe here. We—"

"I know, I know." Nick cut him off. "I just didn't know what else to say or suggest. Fuck, this sucks."

Nick grabbed the phone and dialed Scott's cell. He got the voicemail recording and slammed the phone down again.

"We can't do anything right now. Let's just go to sleep... It'll work itself out. Or we'll figure something out. Either way, right here—right now—we're useless."

Nick stared at Jerry incomprehensively. He understood the logic, but the source puzzled him. Nick wondered if the ordeal was starting to take a toll on Jerry. He nodded and went to check the situation with the boys. Sarah met him in the hallway.

"The boys are in bed. I think they've both calmed down but you'll probably want to talk to them in the morning."

"Thanks Sare..."

"Hey, what are aunties for if not to rescue small children?" She smiled and offered him a hug. He thought it was just to end a bad day, but felt something in it, something he wanted to call forgiveness and hoped this meant she'd moved past his pre-nuptial tantrum. She kissed his cheek and whispered in his ear, confirming his hopes, "It's ok, bro. You were only doing what you always do—what you think is best for everyone." She smiled and sidestepped into her makeshift bedroom, quietly shutting the door behind her.

Jerry was still pacing when Nick returned to the living room to douse lights.

Hunter's outbursts became more frequent after that night, and Tyler became more withdrawn. Sarah involved Tyler with the care of Emily to keep his mind occupied and left Hunter to his father, suggesting he should know how to deal with a miniature version of himself. Scott called back several days later to let them know he'd be staying there and toughing it out. He was afraid the blood spattered on Michelle may have infected her and didn't want to bring it to them. Nick said they understood, but their door was always open if Scott changed his mind. Nick was still reeling from the situation when he and Jerry headed out for supplies.

"When we're done today, can we swing by the house? Sarah wants me to grab everything in the kitchen cupboard—paper plates and spices and whatnot."

Nick nodded while he steered past the debris in the street to leave his neighborhood. "Whatever. Why didn't you get them all before? She grabbed photo albums, why not food? Christ my sister can be brainless some days."

"Hey now. She grabbed the food, this is the nonfood stuff—and I think I may have some chew in the garage I'd like to grab, too. So it's not just her, it's me. And what the hell is up with you?"

"What's up? We're trying to survive and she's worried about paper plates."

"No. I know you better than that. This isn't about Sarah, this is you. What the hell's gotten into you? You've been a fucking bear since... Is this because of Scott?"

"Yes. Well, no. It's just... everything. Are you blind? Look at this place." He jutted his chin toward the windshield, indicating the road ahead of them. Garbage cans had been knocked over, lawns needed cutting, laundry that had been outside when the panic hit was still hanging or lying on the ground, forgotten. "If the plastic on the windows didn't move so they could gawk at us, you'd think it was a ghost town."

"We run into people sometimes…"

"Yeah, people that avoid us. People that won't talk to you because you might be diseased. People that will grab what they want and run away as if you were a leper trying to kiss them."

"Nick, really? It's not all that bad. You have to understand how they feel. Hell, how are we any better? We're covered head to toe, sprayed down with this foul shit—which by the way, is starting to burn a hole right through my damn wrist—and we're not exactly planning any barbeque parties."

"Never mind. You're too thick to get it." Nick watched the house on the corner rather than the road in front of him as they passed it. The house was abandoned now and he made a mental note to check it on one of their excursions to see if they'd left anything useful behind.

Jamie had told him how the woman—who had moved in with her husband, children and home daycare business only a few months before the world ended—had had a hell of a time when all the kids were pulled from her care. Then her own children fell to the dangers of the tiny killers and she learned what Hell really was.

According to a tearful Jamie, several days before the guys returned from their trip, the woman's daughter had been playing with their youngest, Tyler, when Jamie noticed the swollen nodule on the girl's jaw line. Upon closer inspection she quickly sent the girl home and immediately bathed Tyler in water a touch too hot for his comfort. She said she had cried about it that night, and tears welled up again as she repeated the story to Nick, worried she could have hurt Tyler but feeling justified when he remained disease-free. Her guilt resurfaced several days later, when the little girl died and the mother told the press she noticed the sore a full day after Jamie had sent the child home. What if she'd called the mother? Would earlier treatment have helped the girl? Jamie didn't sleep for several days thinking about the possibilities and her part in the child's death. When officials announced none of the serums they had seemed to be having any affect on the infected, Jamie finally slept. Her stomach twisted in guilt, but her mind assured her that once infected, no amount of warning would have helped the girl or her mother.

They pulled into the hospital parking lot, planning on raiding the maintenance area for tools, and Nick turned off the truck after coming to a stop in the emergency lane. Without the engine, the silence of their speechless trip was overwhelming.

"Sorry. It just bugs me to see everyone like this."

"It's ok.—"

"No, it's not." Nick slammed the door as he exited the vehicle. "Remember when 9/11 happened? Afterward there was this amazing communal feeling across the country. This time? No one cares about anyone outside their own house. It's wrong."

"It different, that's all. It's…" Jerry stopped and raised an arm, pointing at the hospital like a mute zombie. "What the hell is that?"

A thick chain was wrapped around the handles of the hospital doors several times and held in place with three different padlocks. Inside, plastic had been fortified with sheets of plywood and windows were blackened with dark tarps.

Nick squinted at the hand written sign on the outside of the glass, "What's that say?"

Jerry took several steps forward, "Closed. But I can't

read what's underneath."

With matching strides, they walked the remaining twenty yards to the hospital's door and read the handwritten sign.

"Shit," Jerry turned and headed back for the truck.

"Bullshit!" Nick kicked the glass door, cracking the tempered glass but gaining no entrance. "Damn it."

"Nick. Come on, man. We still gotta go to my house and I don't want to be out here any longer than we have to."

Through the business district, neither man said anything, but when a young girl who looked like she should have been in the hospital crossed the street in front of them without looking, Nick let loose.

"We apologize for the inconvenience? Are they serious? Where are people supposed to go for medical care? We're all on our own to do the best we can with our first-aid kits? Tell me how this isn't bullshit."

"Oh, I can't. I just don't see how you getting all worked up is going to change any of it." Jerry smirked and tried to break Nick's anger, "You thought a tantrum would stop me from marrying your sister, too. That didn't work out so well either, did it?"

Nick rolled his eyes and offered a fake grin. He stared at Jerry, waiting for more attempts to lighten his mood. Instead Jerry screamed and put his hands against the dash.

"Nick!"

Nick looked forward in time to register the infected deer and slam on the brakes. They screeched to a halt with only a foot to spare between them and the animal.

"Holy crap." Jerry hissed through his teeth.

"Ta hell? It's not even close to dusk. They're just going

to roam town now?"

"Screw it. Go around it. Let's get this done and get back to your house."

After only a few more trips out of the house, they realized their town had been completely ransacked of essentials and began traveling to neighboring communities and out of the way gas stations. The loneliness Nick felt in town was far worse when they traveled further away. His mood seemed to worsen when they were out of the house, but generally came back around to level by the time the girls let them back in again.

The back entry worked as a decontamination room for both garbage dumps and supply runs. Whenever they returned, they stayed in the small mudroom and listened intently for the sound of flies, watching the wall that faced the kitchen, while someone in the kitchen watched the walls and floor behind the men for signs of insect-sized movement. If there were no signs after an hour, they were allowed in. They generally spent the time talking about the lack of other people on the streets—the homeless and insane were presumed long dead from disease or moved on to other areas—and wondered how other households were fairing. The wait in the entry made the excursions longer and, as the adrenaline of being outdoors wore off, they often entered the kitchen completely exhausted. But for the safety of those in the house, Nick and Jerry never complained about Jamie and Sarah's extreme methods.

The adults in the house slept in shifts and took turns watching baby Emily, worried the one person that couldn't let them know a fly was nearby would be the one bitten. They were wrong.

They didn't know for sure how it happened, but were so dependent on the use of the kitchen door they had to blame the basement for letting in the diseased fly. They had no warning, no buzzing to raise their attention. The temperatures were getting lower and lower, and the flies had stopped flying, stopped buzzing. They had become what had once been a funny nickname for lethargic bluebottles out of season, "walks."

Sarah felt what she never heard, and they all knew what had happened by the way she snapped to attention and stared forward for a moment before slapping her neck and pulling off a smear of black death. She turned to her baby and reached out, fear in her eyes and a trembling acknowledgement causing her hand to shake, before pulling away from Emily.

"No..." She half moaned as comprehension that she could never again hold her own child crossed her features and the other three jumped into action without a word. Nick knew his silence was based on cautious fear he might say something to upset her, but figured Jerry's was pure terror and Jamie's was something akin to speechless sympathy.

The bite was treated with rubbing alcohol, searing heat, and another round of alcohol that stung the newly burned flesh and made Sarah scream out in agony, startling the children into tears. She didn't get nauseous for a full twenty-four hours and the other three whispered in hopeful circles outside of her earshot, perhaps it hadn't been a contaminated fly. Unfortunately, the nausea was quickly considered a symptom, as the red spot on her neck turned into a blister with a white halo.

They knew.

She knew.

It was just a matter of time.

They cared for her the best they could, through rubber

gloves and generously lathered layers of hand sanitizer which had been procured on a midnight run to break into the hospital, grocery store and local discount stores for anything and everything they thought might help. The bathroom became a supply closet any M.A.S.H. unit would be proud to call their own, but eventually they came to grips with the fact none of their stolen first-aid would stop her death, or prevent their own. Their survival meant abandoning her.

"We can't kick her out." Jamie tried to let both Sarah's husband and brother know she wasn't suggesting a heartless exile for the girl that had become more than a sister-in-law to her. "But she's a danger. Even if you ignore the danger to us, you have to agree she's a threat to the children."

"What would you suggest? Should we push her out the door and slam it behind her? Or ask nicely if she'd take these supplies and kindly get the fuck out?" Nick barked at his wife under his breath, his furrowed scowl replacing the volume he denied himself for the sake of Sarah, sleeping in the other room.

"She'll never leave Emily." Jerry's comments were matter of fact. The anger rose behind his eyes, but Nick watched as the anger met with worry and frustration for the truths Jamie spoke and mingled to become something of a deadpan tone.

"No. You're not listening." Jamie slumped against the counter, defeat pulling her shoulders into a defiant slouch. "I'm not suggesting we do anything, I'm asking if we should. And if so… What?"

"But even the suggestion…"

"No, Nick. She's right." Jerry looked out the kitchen doorway and Nick knew his brother-in-law could see the children coloring quietly, oblivious to the disease that slept only a few feet away on the couch. "We can't risk the children. We just can't. We can't have made it this far just to endanger, or worse, lose them."

"Jerry—"

"Don't Nick. I know you haven't always liked me, or thought I had your sister's best interests at heart, but we moved beyond all that. This isn't that. This is something uniquely different. This is Emily and Hunter and Tyler."

Jamie reached out and put a hand on his shoulder. "I'm sorry for bringing it up."

"Don't be." He didn't look at her. Instead he stared at Nick. "Seriously, Nick. If this was you... If you were the one out there popping infectious blisters and coughing into the air your children are breathing, what would you do?"

"I'd leave. But that's me, not my sister. I'm a man, I can care for myself and protect myself from the loonies we all know are hiding outside—even though we haven't seen them, we both know they're out there. Not to mention the wild animals that have started cruising through town."

"How about the garage?" Sarah's voice startled them and they turned in unison to see her tear-streaked face. Nick wondered how much his sister had heard and wanted to shrink back into the wall, disappear and pretend the conversation had never happened.

"It's ok. Really." She tried to hold back a cough while she spoke and her voice cracked in response. "I've been thinking about it and I'm surprised you haven't had this conversation before now. I can't stay here. We all know this. But as Nick pointed out, I can't exactly roam the streets. So why not the garage?"

"If you get better then you're still right here and can

come back in—"

"Nicky, I'm not getting better. I'm getting worse and we know where worse leads. Stop trying to hide from the truth and stop trying to protect me. Better me than one of the kids, and I need to leave before it becomes one of the kids. I've been here far too long already."

The room fell silent as they thought about her suggestion and the situation and listened to the giggles of innocence from the other room. Jamie turned and started putting away the dishes from supper. Jerry shifted his weight from one foot to the other in a rhythmic pattern that mimicked his eye movements across the floor, incapable of looking up at his wife. Nick switched his focus from person to person in the room, taking in their actions, or lack thereof, and trying to accept it was no longer their decision. Sarah had made up her mind to leave, and he knew his sister would do it with or without their help or blessing. He finally broke the silence, sighing as he stood up.

"Okay. So what do you need?"

They scattered through the house and gathered a small box of supplies for Sarah. When they met back at the kitchen, Sarah pulled the food from the box.

"I haven't kept anything down for two days. I just hadn't told you. There's no point in me taking food from your mouths. I try to leave the room before I have a coughing fit that ends in bloody rags. And you have no idea how many sores are hidden beneath my clothes. It's bad guys, don't feel guilty." They acknowledged the truth of how advanced the disease was inside her with a mutual silence. "I'll sleep on the couch tonight and spend one last night watching the kids play, and I'll leave in the morning before they're awake so I don't have to deal with them seeing me leave."

The group settled back into the living room with the children, though rather than a normal night of them trying to fill the empty air with movie quotes or book discussions, they sat in silence. Having told them how sick she was, Sarah didn't leave the room to cough and they witnessed something that should have been coming from a lifelong smoker of eighty-five or better, rather than the young woman with the toddler. None of them said a word in response to her hacking. She didn't either. She couldn't meet Nick's worried gaze and only offered an apologetic look to Jerry.

Once the children had fallen asleep to their hundredth viewing of the Spongebob movie and were moved to their beds, the adults began talking quietly. They took turns reliving their children's births and lives, telling stories about Sarah. Several of the tales were funny, but no one laughed. Sarah coughed sporadically and fell asleep twice, only to wake and find them still huddled around her, talking in whispers of days gone by. Sometime around one o'clock in the morning, Nick realized they were holding a wake for someone not yet dead.

"I'm sorry." The whisper from the dark took Nick off guard as he exited the bathroom.

"Sarah? What's wrong?"

"I need you to know two things." Her voice cracked and he wished he could see her better, but she was nothing but a vaguely black outline against a darkened hallway, as his eyes hadn't adjusted from being in the bathroom light.

"Okay..."

"First, I forgive you." Nick smiled in the dark and hoped her eyes had adjusted enough for him to see it. "I forgave you long ago, I'm just stubborn and wanted to hurt you back. I shouldn't have done that. I'm sorry." A half chuckled escaped her between several mild coughs. "In retrospect I was acting as childish as the behavior that had angered me in the first place. Sorry."

"Hon, don't worry about it." He couldn't fathom discussing this when things were as bad as they were and just wanted to accept her admission and move on. "The second thing?"

"I'm pregnant." She whispered so softly he thought he had heard her wrong, but her silence let him know she had actually uttered that and was waiting for his response.

"Sare..." He heard her words again, the sadness that was masked in the whisper and realized the gravity of her illness.

"You can't tell Jerry. Don't tell Jamie either. I only told you because I fear animals tearing me apart once I'm dead and everyone seeing it... Seeing something horrible that will haunt them forever."

"But... How far? When did you find out?"

"I didn't confirm. How could I? There are no doctors and I couldn't ask you guys to pick up a home pregnancy test—we didn't need this with everything going on and I didn't want to stress anyone out. I missed my period right before you guys left, but I used to miss in the summer all the time, so I didn't think anything of it. I missed when you returned and I figured it was stress. Then I missed another and little symptoms started popping up. My breasts are killing me, the flutters have begun. Yeah, I'm pregnant. I know what it feels like."

"Ok... But why tell me? What do you want—"

"You need to burn me."

"What?"

"When I die. You need to burn me. Don't bury me or leave me anywhere. I don't want animals digging me up or tearing me apart. You need to burn me, for my own sanity, for everyone else's. No one can see anything that may upset them, that might let them know I was pregnant."

"Hon, you being dead will be upsetting. You being..." He couldn't bring himself to repeat the horrible possibilities she'd uttered. "...animals getting to you, would be upsetting. How could— ?"

"Please. Just promise me. I don't know how long I'll make it in the garage. I'm cough blood, covered in sores and hurt in ways and places I didn't know possible. Just promise... ok?"

"Okay..."

A few hours of sleep later, they woke to Nick's watch alarm and prepared to move Sarah. Finding she'd died during the interim stunned them, but knowing the children would be awake soon offered them no time to mourn and barely enough time to register the fact. They needed to deal with the situation and simply tell the children what had happened, rather than have the kids wake up to a body. Reality was harsh at that age, but it didn't need to be in their face.

After a very brief discussion on whether she should be buried or taken to another part of town—after all, death brings flies and they didn't need to invite them with a meal—Nick convinced the others it was best to burn her body. There would be no visitation, funeral, or even an announcement in the paper, just a tarp and thick smoke. Nick had planned to do it in the backyard, keeping it as private as he could, but Jamie disagreed.

"It's as close to a funeral as we're going to have, and I'd like to be there, or at least see it from the window. I don't know if Jerry will or not, if he'll even be able to, but if he wants to, he can watch if you do it in the street." Nick acquiesced with a nod and began to suit up for the trip outdoors.

Sarah's death occurred at what would normally have been the week of Thanksgiving. But normal had come and gone months before, leaving them with no turkey and football to garnish the meal with family and friends. Instead, Nick bundled up against the cold of Wisconsin's brutal winter and dragged his sister's corpse to the curb with a duty-bound numbness that equated to taking out the garbage. He left her there, unattended, to get two pallets from the garage, peripherally aware of the gaps in the plastic of the houses around him. He and Jerry had seen that before, the little movements in window coverings, and while they usually waved with a silliness meant to alleviate the stress of being outdoors, Nick did nothing more than glance at the curious as he prepared the funeral pyre.

A few squirts of highly flammable brake fluid and the pallets lit with ease. The goggles worn to protect him from rogue flies kept the smoke out of his eyes, but the scarf wrapped around his face did nothing to protect him from the smell as the flame touched flesh. He watched the flame on the wood, rather than the melting plastic of the old blue tarp. He thought of his summers spent at their grandparents' house harassing his sister until she told Grandma and got him grounded, and his first semester at college, when he'd drunk dialed Sarah on a regular basis under the pretense of alcohol and fraternity pranks but knowing full well he missed the one person who knew all his dirty secrets and loved him anyway. He tried not to cry and fill the goggles with tears as he said good-bye to the girl who had only given up her slingshot because it didn't fit in her pocket next to the bulk of her baby's bottle. He thought of their last whispered conversation and the knowledge only he knew, and hoped the flame would hide any evidence of the truth. Hoped that fulfilling his promise would protect those she'd wanted protected.

His eyes roamed without seeing across the melting tarp and exposed, blackened flesh of the body he'd depersonalized for his own sanity. The white gleam of bone shone through flames on occasion, quickly darkening as soot and scorch charred it, but it was just bone, not his sister. The gore that spilled and bubbled once the skin and muscle were breached was nothing of the person he remembered, but something surreal his mind equated to tragedy on the evening news. Removed. Someone else. Somewhere else.

So content in his thick quagmire of memories, fooling himself into believing he was breathing brisk winter air, rather than death choked oxygen, Nick didn't see the person leave the house across the street. And he wouldn't have noticed another mourner, had the man not kicked up the sparks and shifted the balance of the charring pallets with a tarp-wrapped body of his own.

Nick jumped at the disturbance and looked up at the intruder. Wearing a full snowsuit and a snorkeling mask, the interloper was the epitome of a "made for Sci-Fi" cast member. But the duct tape covered joints between snowsuit and boot, and snowsuit and leather gloves, combined with the neoprene neck cover, let Nick know instantly this man had also been out of the house to forage. This was his battle suit.

Because he had not seen which house the man had come from, Nick wasn't sure which neighbor was sharing his bonfire, combining their tragedies in early morning silence. He studied the man across the fire. The flickering flames reflected off the plastic of the mask, but Nick looked past to find the man's eyes. It took several moments for Nick to recognize the forty-something neighbor from the corner. The mask had prevented him—Thompson or Johnson, one of those "son" names—from wearing his glasses and made it more difficult for Nick to figure out who it was.

Nick was surprised he had deduced it out from the man's eyes alone. The man was a stranger to Nick, barely more than the guy you saw at the grocery store from time to time and then recognized elsewhere but couldn't place him.

The man and his wife had moved into the house on the opposite corner almost three years ago, yet for whatever reason, Nick and Jamie had never walked across to welcome them to the neighborhood. The couple had no children, so there was no reason for his boys to play over there and force an introduction. They had no animals that wandered off the property and had to be called for, searched for, or brought back to the house you knew they belonged to. There had been no inclination to get to know the couple.

Nick thought about this, almost ashamed he had never bothered to say hello.

Glad for the thought distracting his attention from the body lying in front of him, Nick let his mind wander on the tangent of society's solitary lifestyle. Gone were the days of his childhood when his mother would welcome new neighbors with fresh baked goods and a friendly smile. This was a new century and a new mindset. If he didn't know them or have reason to know them, he didn't go out of his way. Likewise, he didn't get involved if they needed help, and no foraging committees had been created in the neighborhood.

In the face of disease and tragedy, the neighborhood had boarded itself up. Individual strongholds were formed, with loved ones and friends, instead of a communal gathering at a church or school. Sure the town had tried, but without trust you have nothing and without communication with the outside world, there was no telling if they were any better or worse than other areas—mentally or physically. But standing in the middle of the street, watching the remains of his sister and a stranger's loved one, burn in silence, Nick had an urge to go check on other people. He had a craving to know his town, not just his family, was safely tucked inside—whether it be in small groups or larger gatherings.

Instead, he stoically remained where he was, reflecting on the fact that society had, in only a few generations, moved from a community where people knew each other to small intimate collectives, which blocked out the rest of the world. It wasn't just him, no one mingled on the corners or visited across the fences anymore. They emailed and talked on the Internet, in chatrooms and message boards where they knew before entering there would be a shared interest. There was no need for small talk to find out what he had in common with his neighbor. There was no wandering across the street to help someone work on their car or chat while the other barbequed.

Nick realized the larger a community became, the more tribal and closed its inhabitants were. If society was going to survive, it was going to have to open itself back up. People needed to embrace the fact they were not alone behind their boarded windows and snorkel masks. And in the glow of his sister's death, he informally met his neighbor with nothing more than a nod of acceptance.

The flames died down as the fuel—both wood and woman—burned away. Neither man ever said a word, but as anxiety shifted their weight from foot to foot they had managed to gradually move from standing across each from each other to standing next to each other. Nick wondered if it was the man's wife or a friend burning next to his sister. However, since he couldn't bring himself to offer sympathetic condolences, he decided not to query about the body wrapped in the tarp. As the flames became embers they nodded to each other and returned to their prospective homes—a newfound wealth of understanding and camaraderie in Nick's heart and mind.

When Jerry snapped out of his trance-like state several days later, he was a changed person. There were no more hunting stories or inappropriate jokes to lighten the mood. He was no longer the reluctant clown responsible for keeping spirits up and carried everyone along by pretending nothing was wrong. He was now the vigilant survivor who checked the windows and doors and vents several times a day—nearly beginning his rounds over again just as soon as he'd finished the last sweep. He never let Emily out of his sight, watching her as he worked or carrying her with him to inspect other rooms. He didn't sleep more than three hours at a time, and even that was always during the day when others were awake. Within a month he was as removed from his former self as a cancer patient is in their last few weeks. It would have annoyed Nick, as Sarah had been his sister much longer than she'd been Jerry's wife, had Jerry's vigilant behavior not proven to be useful when the wild animals wandering town started to become a threat.

They'd first noticed the infected coyote and other wildlife wandering the streets right before Christmas, when Jamie had sent them out to the local toy store under the charade of forced normalcy and presents for the children. Looking mangy, if not manic, the animals knocked over long rotted garbage cans and nosed through the remains that lay in piles of snow-covered ash in the streets. It seemed to be only larger mammals, and they decided the squirrels and other small creatures they'd initially seen in the streets had most likely succumbed to the disease quicker because of their size, or become food for the other animals. Jamie mentioned she hadn't seen a bird since the first snowfall, quickly pointing out that not every single bird was known to migrate, so they assumed those that stayed behind had all died. The family pets had left the neighborhoods long ago, and ironically seemed to trade places with the animals that normally lived in the surrounding woods. The coyotes seemed to be the most commonly spotted, whether Nick and Jerry were off foraging through town or peaking out their own windows. When the coyotes seemed to disappear overnight, they should have known there was a reason other than just disease. There was no way it had killed the entire pack in one day.

One thing about wild packs Nick had always found interesting was that coyotes were terrified of wolves. Humans had been creating monsters out of them for centuries, most notably Red Riding Hood and werewolves, but really had no modern cause for concern. Wolves never entered town. Sure an occasional bear would get stuck in a tree at the park, or a raccoon would be caught in a live trap and returned to the woods rather than left to hang out in a garage, but wolves were more afraid of humans and less interested in getting over that for the sake of food.

Or at least they were until they got sick.

While Sarah had seemed to have all her faculties right up until the end, Nick had to believe the animals were affected differently. The snarling and baying held no romantic quality in the empty streets. It was nothing short of menacing after sundown. And the night the infected pack figured out the smells of food came from behind the barricaded windows, a nightmarish fairytale came to life.

The first scream woke Nick. It took him a second to figure out why he was awake in the first place and he mentally checked off a list of possibilities: need to piss, nightmare, kid by the bed tugging on him—nope. Then he heard the second scream and leapt from the covers. Within moments he was at the door to the boys' room, but they were tucked in and sleeping soundly. The lump that was Emily under her Winnie the Pooh blanket moved with rhythmic breaths and he knew she was still happily unconscious. He closed the door and headed down the hall toward the living room.

"Shhhh…" Jerry's voice came from somewhere behind the flashlight which blinded Nick unexpectedly.

"What the hell was that?" Nick whispered and joined his brother-in-law.

"Wolves."

"But it sounded like a scream. Bobcats sound like that, not wolves."

"No. Wolves attacking humans. You heard the humans." Jerry turned away and went to the window.

Nick didn't mind the vigilance Jerry had taken on

after the death of Sarah, but the truncated sentences were annoying. He felt like he was trying to get information from a teenager that didn't understand they should just tell you the whole story, with full sentences, rather than make you keep asking for the next portion. He huffed under his breath and prepared to start the cat and mouse game to get information out of his brother-in-law, when he heard his name whispered.

Jerry extinguished the flashlight and then pulled the duct tape from the peek hole they'd cut out, motioning Nick to come look. "They broke into the house over there a few moments ago."

Nick peered into the moonlit darkness, unsure which house Jerry had referred to until he saw the broken picture window and pacing pack. "How many went in?"

"Two. They banged against the door for a while before taking a stab at the window. When they got in, I heard a gunshot and saw a flash, but since then it's been nothing but screams."

Nick watched the pack pace in the street, obviously agitated or anticipating food, and wondered how long before they would systematically go from picture window to picture window along the block. He didn't have to wait long, as Emily squawked down the hall to announce she'd woken for some apparent reason and the pack turned as one to stare back at him.

A large, exceptionally mangy wolf leapt toward the house and Nick backed up instinctively. Jerry stood his ground and watched the animal for a moment before walking over to the fireplace and grabbing his hunting rifle off the mantel. Nick hadn't noticed it there and wondered whether the 30-06 was new tonight because of the pack, or if Jerry kept it handy every night.

Outside, two more wolves bounded into the snow covered front yard and began to pace in front of them. Nick turned to Jerry. Jerry looked past Nick down the hall to his crying daughter. Without a word, Nick understood. Jerry had the gun and he wasn't giving it up, so Nick turned to attend to his niece and quiet her before the wolves broke in. Unfortunately, he understood Jerry's thoughts a moment too late, and as he took a step toward the hall the window exploded behind him, catching him off guard. Nick dropped to a squat in a reactionary defensive move, twisting him back around to face the danger.

The rifle was deafening in the quiet house and even though Nick hadn't been looking directly at it, he was momentarily blinded. His mind, however, had not been paralyzed, and he lunged at the fireplace, groping for the poker he knew was there, to arm himself in some way against the intruder. When his eyes readjusted he saw the dead wolf lying at the base of the window. Two more used its carcass as a landing pad, as they entered the house and immediately turned toward the small noises Emily continued to make down the hall.

"What the hell?" Nick and Jerry turned at the sound of Jamie's voice. Jerry followed the wolves with the barrel of the gun rather than his eyes. Nick grabbed the flashlight from the table and flashed it down the hall, screaming as he illuminated the danger to his wife.

"Get back!" He saw the white of Jamie's eyes and heard her gasp, as she spun on one foot and sprinted to the bathroom at the end of the hall.

"Shit! Not the bathroom..." Jerry lowered the gun. The wolves chased Jamie and slammed into the door as she shut it behind her. "She's in the line of fire." He glared at Nick and headed toward the hall. Nick peeked outside, checking on the rest of the pack and wondering why they didn't all follow into the houses to feed, before remembering pecking order ruled wild canines at mealtime.

The snarling wolves banged against the bathroom door. Jamie's screams behind it muffled Emily's cries. "Kill them!" She hollered over and over, and Nick could imagine her flinching every time the wolves slammed against the door. He was impressed the door hadn't crumbled yet, as he didn't think the interior doors of the house were sturdy enough to ward off a determined attack, and he wondered if Jamie was pushed up against it to give it added strength.

"Shoot them." Nick whispered to Jerry, pleading for him to either deal with the situation or hand over the gun. Nick's own gun was in the bedroom, but the wolves were between him and it, and he wished he had grabbed it when he'd jumped out of bed. Cursing himself, he urged Jerry to act, "Shoot them, for God's sake."

Jerry nodded and aimed low at the first wolf's form. Nick saw his eyes glance up at the door and wondered if he were gauging where Jamie was standing. He watched Jerry finger the trigger and knew they'd only have one shot to do this right before the wolves likely turned their attention back to the men or the bedroom housing the crying meal ticket. He waited a moment, until he was sure Jerry was seconds from firing, and yelled at his wife. "Get in the bathtub!"

The shot was deafening. The yelp was unmistakably pain. The crash behind the door was followed by a muffled vulgarity.

The bullet had entered the wolf's spine just as it

had slammed into the door. As it slid to the ground in a lifeless pile, its blood smeared the cracked door. The second wolf turned and snarled at them. Nick realized they blocked its exit and raised the fire poker above his head, readying for the attack. Instead, the animal turned back to the door. Either the disease had ruined his mind and he was unaware of the danger above his hunger, or he believed the door was a way out. Ignoring the other wolf, the second one rammed into the door as Jerry took aim. With Jamie's body no longer bracing it on the other side, it began to crack and give. In all the commotion, the little noises seemed louder than they should to Nick, as they represented his wife's safety being shattered.

The blast caught the wolf just as the door gave way. His body tumbled through the shattered wood and veneer and skidded to a halt at the base of the bathtub. Jamie jumped up, holding the shower rod above her like a spear, and stared at the bloody mess until Nick's voice broke her concentration.

"Jamie?"

She blinked and looked up at him before crumbling to the cold porcelain. Her shaking was visible to Nick, even in the dim hallway and he put a hand on Jerry's shoulder to get past him. Jerry turned around to face Nick but his eyes stopped to the side of him. Nick followed Jerry's gaze and saw Hunter standing in his bedroom doorway. Nick took a step toward the room and stopped.

Hunter stood, his legs spread in a sturdy half squat, the innocence of his crumpled Batman pajamas offsetting the seriousness in his face. The thin, Lord of the Rings toy sword he had gotten for his last birthday was held above his head with the white knuckles of his right hand. His left hand was braced against the doorframe. Steady.

Equally white from pressure. His stance was protection, or at least the best imitation a seven-year-old could offer. No one, or thing, was getting into that room without going through him.

Behind Hunter, his younger brother Tyler huddled underneath the crib. The boy gripped Emily firmly in the six-year-old safety of his arms. He had her Pooh blanket wrapped around her for the dual purpose of added protection and comfort, and his eyes mirrored her own, the fear palpable in the silent tears that ran down his face. None of the children spoke. None had screamed. They were scared silent and even though the commotion had passed, they were frozen as such.

Forgetting about Jamie for a moment, Nick sidestepped to his son and gently tried to pull the sword from his hand. Hunter looked up at him with a lost expression and he could tell the boy didn't know if he truly believed it was over. If it was really safe. Nick tugged at the sword, watching the boy's eyes the entire time. Hunter finally released the sword, as his eyes came into focus on his father's face, and Nick set it on the carpet. He pulled his son's other hand from the door jam and gathered the boy in his arms.

"It's ok, Hunter. It's over now."

Jamie had come from the bathroom and now pushed past the two in the doorway, Jerry right behind her, to retrieve the other children from under the crib. From the hallway, Hunter's voice cracked, barely above a whisper.

"No it's not. The rest of them are still out there. I can hear them." Over the boy's shoulder, Nick made eye contact with Jamie and Jerry. Jerry nodded and handed Emily to Jamie before he popped open the rifle and reloaded it as he left the room.

"You stay in here with mommy. Daddy and Uncle Jerry will take care of this and be right back." Nick urged Jamie with his eyes to come get Hunter and she read the request without question. She pulled the boy into the room and shut the door. Nick heard what sounded like the dresser being dragged in front of the door and frowned. He supposed she had had enough with broken doors and wasn't letting anything back into that room until she knew it was safe.

Jerry stood by the window, watching the diminished pack from the edge of broken glass and flapping plastic.

"Where'd they all go?" Nick asked as he joined his brother-in-law.

"To the next house or block or neighborhood, I imagine."

"Is it over then?"

"Not as long as this window is open, and the others are available. We can't sit here waiting for them to die."

"What do you want to do?"

"We've got to board it up. Board them all up. Do we have any planks or anything in the garage?"

"There's one pallet left we could tear apart and use, but other than that…" The living room was barely visible in the moonlight that seeped through the broken window, but he perused its shadows for an answer.

"Doors." Jerry set the rifle on the fireplace mantel and grabbed the tobacco tin from his back pocket. Nick knew Jerry's nicotine supply was getting low but the dip was a requirement after the stressful events. "We'll use the interior doors."

Nick and Jerry quickly took the doors off the closets of the house, leaving the bedroom doors for a touch of protection and privacy, and nailed them up over the picture window frame. The shorter planks from the pallets and cupboard doors from the kitchen were used to cover the smaller windows. When they were done, Nick felt they were more fortified, but was too on edge to relax quite yet. He quietly accepted the sting in his chest, as he became even more isolated from the rest of the world.

Cabin fever hit full force just about the time Nick and the others began to hear phantom buzzing. To be honest, Nick hadn't heard any buzzing for several months, and the lethargic winter-version of the flies had only been around for a few weeks after Sarah's death. When they vanished, when the physical evidence of the flies was gone, everyone began to imagine the insect everywhere. It was as if the silence bred fear and initiated waking nightmares. Nick blamed the imagined fear for the very real mental breakdowns that began spreading through his house, and the town at large.

People were still getting sick, as the nature of the disease was contagion, not just the fly bites. Bodies were still being dumped in the middle of streets and burned—Jamie assumed they had been all along, but Nick hadn't noticed it in his own neighborhood until the morning he'd done it himself. And in the silence of the pre-dawn light, late one day in January, the emotionally unstable tipped over to the other side of the scales and began acting up as if a remote had been triggered, causing them all to snap in rapid succession—a domino effect of insanity.

The three of them watched as people ran down the streets batting at swarms that didn't exist. Children, presumed to have lost their parents and been trapped indoors with the bodies, clawed their way through boards and plastic to run wild through the streets. Parents with lost children, or adults in general who had lost hope, walked outside unprotected from either element or disease, and looked for death to take away their pain. On their supply run, Nick and Jerry saw what looked like patients in hospital gowns wandering about, knocking on random doors, and leaving a wake of terrified people in their path. Word on the rumor board—the front window of the grocery story, which had become a hot spot for people to post notes to other scavengers—claimed the homeless had been responsible for burning down businesses and at least three residential blocks in the name of infestation.

Society had broken down, but not in any way Nick had ever read about in apocalyptic thrillers. Rather than turning to criminals with tribal instincts and territorial demeanors, people withdrew. They locked their doors and never came out. The only people who ever made it outside were the dead and the crazy. And Nick and Jerry, who presumed there must be others still foraging, but had stopped seeing them or the evidence they left behind. Fear had locked doors and closed hearts. No one cared to help each other, not even to rescue a frightened child from the streets. Sole survival wasn't just an instinct anymore; it was a way of life. And as the realization hit Nick, the power went out and left them in the dark.

That was the state of things three months ago. Two months ago, the cold killed off most of those wandering the streets or lacking alternative heat sources for their homes. Nick and Jerry foraged for wood to burn in the fireplace whenever they left the house for food, often resorting to physically tearing apart empty houses to keep their own home warm. The generator they had secured back in September had been declared emergency only, since they couldn't run down to the gas station for more fuel. They'd only used it when the temperatures dropped too far below zero to make gathering firewood possible, and even then used it only to power space heaters. The butane stove only lasted a few weeks for meals and then they began to cook over the open flame of the fireplace. On a good day, they could find some humor and consider it an extended camping trip while they filled jugs at the artesian wells. On a bad day, the house was quiet. Not even the children spoke as they wandered aimlessly through the activities of their, now normal, day-to-day lives.

A month ago, Nick had realized they were simply sitting around waiting to die. He knew when winter ended, so too would the reprieve from the flies. At the time it was mid-February, and in northern Wisconsin, the coldest part of winter. But they all knew what came next. First they would experience the false spring that could, if it got warm enough, bring flies back. That would be followed by anywhere from a few weeks to another month or two of winter, always including at least one blizzard, before true spring started poking its nose around. The flies were coming back. Nick could see it in their eyes; they just didn't say it out loud. What they did acknowledge was the need for a plan.

The plan was simple: find somewhere safe. The problem was, with no communications left, they didn't know where safe was. Without the television or phones or radios, they didn't know how far it had spread or how dangerous other communities had become. They knew nothing. They based their discussions on what they did know—the tiniest danger, which posed the biggest threat.

"Even in Alaska they have a brief summer, and

summer brings flies." Jerry spoke from the kitchen as they discussed their options. He busied himself by making a list of their remaining provisions and another list of what they'd need to procure for their trip.

"Equator jumping?" Jamie suggested. Nick answered her with a blank stare. "You know, we drive to wherever winter is. North in the fall, below the border in the spring."

"That's a lot of traveling." Nick tried to imagine the six of them packed into her SUV with all their supplies and provisions. "What about gas? We'd have to refuel, and that would mean getting out of the car."

"Extra gas tanks? Refueling only in cold climates?" She stared at the ground. "I don't know."

"Oh hey, wait..." Jerry's voice from the kitchen had something Nick hadn't heard for months—hope—and Nick sat up as Jerry filled empty doorway. "You still have that trailer out behind the shed?"

"Yeah."

"Not a problem then, and not a bad idea at all, Jamie." He smiled and put down the pad of paper. "I'm going to need some things."

Nick knew exactly where he was going with this thought, and as it panned out, first vocally, then on paper, and finally in the act of scavenging gas tanks from anything nearby, he wasn't sure he believed in the possibility. Could it really be that easy? Calculating the drive to be at least a week, and more likely two, each direction, he didn't like their odds of having enough gas and food. But the plan had given hope to both his friend and his wife, and their renewed spirit was infectious, improving the demeanor of all three children, even though Emily wasn't old enough to understand they'd been in a bad mood. Deciding he'd rather die happy than cranky, Nick didn't voice his objections and went along with their plan. Any plan was better than giving up and waiting for death to return with the melting snow.

Jerry spent the next three weeks welding a complex pile of tanks and tubes to each other and then the trailer, as he created a moving gas station for them. Jamie packed and shopped—if it could be called shopping when you take it for free from the homes of the dead. Nick busied himself by siphoning gas from the vehicles Jerry hadn't taken the tanks from, Jerry promising to dump whatever gas was left in the generator into the tanks, as soon as he was done welding. The three of them walked in and out of the house without fear, certain there were no flies in the winter and therefore no danger. They were met with odd looks through curtains, faces pressed against barrier plastic to watch, and were sure to be the gossip of the neighborhood—if it could still be called gossip when confined to each household. Nick half expected other neighbors to inquire, if not join in on the escape plan. They did neither.

Nick felt anger building behind his fear. They were supposed to be leaving this morning. They were supposed to be safely on the road, behind rolled up windows, before the flies returned. They were not supposed to die here, at the hands of the disease buzzing from the kitchen.

He tightened his grip on the flyswatter and walked through the doorway to the kitchen. The garbage had begun to pile in the corner, the winter's lack of flies combined with their travel preparations had taken so much of their time lately it had caused them to grow lazy. He blamed the garbage for attracting the small carrier of death that roamed somewhere in the room that was once filled with memories of his boys and their afternoon snacks, family meals, and holiday breakfasts.

The buzzing stopped and Nick froze. He needed the fly to make noise. Without electricity, without lights, he knew he'd never find it by sight in the early morning light. He never thought he'd want to hear another fly's wings rapidly declaring their position, but he did now.

What if he hadn't really heard it? What if the anticipation of leaving had caused a brief return of the phantom buzzing that had plagued them earlier in winter?

The buzzing resumed and Nick was torn between joy and anxiety.

It echoed oddly and Nick looked around the small room trying to make sense of the noise. When he turned to his left, it got louder, so he cautiously took two steps toward it.

The buzzing stopped.

"Damn it." His grip on the metal handle of the swatter tightened in frustration and the wire dug into his flesh. He was about to declare himself one of the insane when the buzzing began again and he pinpointed its location—the sink.

Walking slowly across the linoleum to stay quiet and be able to hear the soft echo of the noise, he made his way to the stainless steel double basin on the left wall. The window above it had been sealed months ago, the plastic covering the wood appeared intact, the duct tape around it unblemished. Where did the fly come from? Up from the basement again? Snuck in with them? Mysteriously born of the garbage pile up? Did it matter? After months of surviving and weeks of planning, death had found a way back into his house.

He stood on his tiptoes and peered into the sink from several feet away, but couldn't locate the fly in either side. He drew closer and the buzzing stopped again. He paused. He was a patient man—he had to be, to keep his sanity while locked inside for over half a year—and he could wait until the fly made noise again.

He relaxed his muscles and lowered himself back to his flat feet, as his eyes flitted back and forth between the side Jamie used to wash and the side she had declared for rinsing only. The faded, hunter green dish strainer in the sink just barely showed over the edge, a relic from when life was normal. Life was anything but normal. If it had been normal, there would be dishes in the sink, a washcloth hanging over the faucet, and a half-empty container of Dawn on the back edge. Instead, dishes were cleaned with baby wipes and then stacked on the counter—the drainer sat alone in the sink, forgotten. When the buzzing started again, Nick realized it was coming from the second side.

A quick step forward, swatter poised overhead, and he looked straight into what was supposed to be Jamie's sanitary side of the sink. The silverware attachment was empty except for a corncob skewer—there always seemed to be one left behind when the dishes were put away. Inspecting the strainer from various angles, Nick could see no fly anywhere and braved moving the strainer. He slipped the flyswatter through the wire slots of the strainer and lifted it from the sink slowly. The buzzing stopped and he abruptly put the strainer down to regain full use of the swatter.

He held his breath and listened. One bite was all it took. One bite to ruin the lives of his wife and children. One bite to make surviving winter a moot point. He stared at the strainer and dared it to grow wings and bristly whiskers and a sharp scissor-like mouth to infect him. The sink drain answered him with lightly echoing buzzing.

The pipes? Was the fly somewhere in the pipes, and the lack of electronics humming in his house made it so quiet he could hear it through the metal pathways traversing behind walls and under floors? Nick peered down into the drain, swatter held near his head for quick intervention.

He immediately sprang back to an upright position. Disbelief swam across his face and he looked back down to the drain, the hand holding the swatter hung at his side. The latticed plastic and wire weapon forgotten.

When he looked up again he laughed. Out loud. Without reservation.

He laughed so hard the sound reverberated throughout the house and he knew he'd awakened the rest of the house by the faint swish of opening doors and confused morning voices.

There in the sink below him, the fly—the little black bringer of fear and destructor of society—had been trapped by the tiniest spider Nick had ever seen spin a web. Unused for so long, the drainer had become the perfect place for a web, and whatever tiny bit of moisture may have been on the metal of the sink, was the perfect lure.

Death had been caught, for the moment.

"What's going on?" Jamie stared at him as Nick held

his stomach. It didn't matter if the peal of laughter had been genuine humor or just an uncomfortable relief, it had been a long time since he'd laughed like that and his muscled ached as if he'd just run a 5k marathon with a hangover.

He met her eyes briefly before he tossed the unused flyswatter at Jerry. Was Mother Nature taking over? Were there enough spiders? Nick smiled at them both, grabbed the box of supplies off the counter, and headed toward the door to load it into the SUV.

"Winter's done. It's time to go."

The story continues...

I didn't initially plan a sequel, but several years later, these people had more to tell. The surviving characters, and the journey they are about to embark on, can be found and followed in the stand-alone sequel titled The Hatch, an excerpt of which is available on the following pages.

Author Note

Waiting Out Winter was spurned by the fact that the DNR did indeed attempt to kill off the tent worm invasion a few years ago by releasing an obscene amount of black flies. Just like the story, they released them a touch too late and rather than fixing the problem, they added to it. While there were no deaths in Northern Wisconsin from biting flies, there was an awful lot of itching, complaining and even cancelled vacations because people couldn't keep them at bay with even the strongest of bug repellants. It's the only year I remember actually looked forward to winter, knowing the flies would finally be gone.

ABOUT THE AUTHOR

Born and raised in Wisconsin, Kelli Owen now lives in Pennsylvania. She's attended countless writing conventions, participated on dozens of panels, and spoken at the CIA Headquarters in Langley, VA. Visit her website at kelliowen.com for more information. F/F

THE
HATCH

(Stand-alone sequel to Waiting Out Winter)

about THE HATCH

Nick Kontis and his remaining family members have survived winter--have outlived the threat of deadly infected flies--and are heading toward presumed safety. They quickly find all exit points blocked, the perimeter burned, and learn the flies were only the beginning, as Mother Nature has stepped in to correct mankind's mistakes.

Her weapon of choice: spiders.

With thick webs covering the spring landscape, and lack of any communication leaving them on their own to guess whether or not the spiders are as lethal as the flies they're eating, they make a new plan. Fleeing in a new direction they run into another party of survivors. And what was once a breakdown of society becomes an exercise in rebuilding.

They'll need to find common ground and bond with the others, before winter arrives again. Before the spiders declare victory...

(see following pages for an excerpt...)

PROLOGUE

I miss the frogs. I don't miss pancakes or Saturday morning cartoons with the boys. No, I miss the fucking frogs.

It was the tent worms, really. Stupid little green caterpillars. You know, the ones people tinfoil their tree trunks against. They changed everything. The way we live. The way we die.

Every ten years or so, the tent worm population booms in the Midwest for a season. Last summer, we had a tent worm outbreak so horrible it made the biblical locusts look like a joke. The religious claimed it was a sign of the end—the eleventh plague. Historians agreed it was unprecedented. Forest management compared the devastation to the Peshtigo fire we'd all learned about in fourth grade but had completely forgotten until they brought it up again. And the scientists, well...the scientists thought they could fix it. Their solution didn't stop the damn tent worms at all. Instead, it brought us a man-made swarm of disease in the form of biting black flies. Infected, contagious—one bite enough to kill you—and they dropped millions.

Man thought it could outsmart Mother Nature. The problem is, mankind has never been quite as smart as it thinks. So we spent the winter holding our breath and waiting to die. Society broke down. Rather than joining together, it became every family for themselves. The seven of us went inside and stayed there. We plugged up every hole in the house, covered windows with boards and plastic, and shut ourselves off from the world—only venturing out for supplies, and even then we were covered head-to-toe in clothes and plastic and chemicals. I lost my sister to a single fucking fly bite. Many of our relatives and close friends didn't make it either—some from flies, others from starvation or suicide. God knows who else died after communications were cut.

I sincerely hope whichever scientist thought releasing those flies was a good idea found out firsthand just how wrong they fucking were. I hope they got bit. I hope they watched in horror as the sores popped up on their body, before breaking open, bleeding and oozing pus all over them and their family. I hope they coughed up so much blood they couldn't remember what anything else had ever tasted like. I hope they suffered and died like so many others bit by the damn flies. No! I hope his children got bit first. I hope he watched, helpless, as those he loved the most were covered in bursting oozing sores of infection. I hope he saw them cough and sputter and cry from pain, and then die. Then, and only then, do I hope he got bit and suffered, and bled, and wheezed all alone into his own death. We'll never know who it was. Dead or alive, they'll never tell us. Probably better that way. But if that bastard survived the flies, I hope to hell he lived through the frogs.

See, Mother Nature hadn't quite given up on us yet, and spring brought frogs to deal with the flies. So many damn frogs.

We had initially thought we could just go south in the spring and north in the fall, hop the equator both ways, and live in a sort of permanent winter until the problem was solved. But the roads were a mess, and we found them blocked off completely just past the Illinois border. Lateral travel showed us blackened woods and the burned out remains of towns between the barricades.

We had heard through the rumor mill of hazmat-suited teams spraying areas, and planes dropping chemicals, but we hadn't heard a peep about them burning down towns and forests. Not a single word of military action except the National Guard being called in. But the evidence was everywhere. And this wasn't just the National Guard. Tanks blocked roadways, barbed wire stretched across all exit points, discarded shell boxes—everything my worst nightmares could conjure.

A full day and a half of traveling the edge of the ash and we realized they must have burned a rough circle around all the infected counties. Northern Illinois, the eastern third of Minnesota, and most of Wisconsin had been quarantined with flame, barricades, and barbed wire. That was enough to stop vehicles from leaving, but then we noticed the bits of body parts on the snow patches and dried grass, and could only guess their back-up plan was landmines to prevent escape by foot. We were being shot by our own, not because of war or even an uprising of civil unrest. No, we were being quarantined and killed by fear.

Jerry said we were lucky they didn't fucking napalm us. At the time, I downplayed the idea because the boys were awake in the back seat—Tyler crying out of anxiety, and Hunter suddenly asking questions. But I knew Jerry had a point. Protocol should have been to wipe us out, flies and humans alike.

I still wonder why they didn't.

I still worry they might.

The option of running away to winter elsewhere was as dead as those we left behind. We spotted army patrols near the perimeter, and without knowing whether or not they had orders to shoot on sight, we avoided them at all costs. Between the armed guard and barricades, we were trapped. We were forced to rethink, regroup.

Our new plan was to head toward the top of Wisconsin, up along Lake Superior. A house or cabin maybe, something with protected well water and a fireplace. In the midst of the pine forests would be perfect. The tent worms didn't eat the pine, so we figured there wouldn't be as many flies there—either existing naturally or delivered like an insect A-Bomb by the idiots last summer.

We stuck to small side roads to avoid the military, but it was slow travel. Sure, we were being cautious, but six months of no upkeep, and the abandoned vehicles blocking our way, sent us in zigzag patterns on back roads and turned a four-hour trip into several long days. Just north of Marshfield we grabbed maps at a forgotten gas station, and found an empty house. We were surrounded by fields rather than woods, and hoped that could mean less flies. We settled in to take a breather while we mapped out a new destination further north.

And then the damn frogs showed up.

At first we were thrilled. We knew the flies had returned. We were back on high alert—covered as much as possible and keeping the children protected. And then we heard the spring peeps. Frogs eat flies. This was excellent news and we cheered them on. Man had allowed his conceit to interfere with nature, and now she was going to fix the problem we had caused. And the frogs came. In droves.

I used to think frogs were cute. I don't know if it was because I grew up in the Kermit generation, or because I could always relate to their strangely graceful awkwardness. When they swarmed the backyard, we watched in delight from the windows. We knew they were taking out whatever flies had survived winter. But when we went on supply runs and they were all over the streets, making the roads slippery with their slime and blood, worse than even the tent worms had been, they started to lose their charm. When they began perching on the windowsills, staring at us through the plastic... yeah, that creeped us out. We heard a croak in the middle of the night once and realized one had gotten inside. We spent hours going over every inch of that house trying to figure out where it had slipped through. Never did figure it out. Didn't have a chance.

There were too many frogs and nature needed to correct itself again.

The birds and snakes announced the official arrival of spring, showing up almost over night and seeming to enjoy their frog buffet. There didn't appear to be more than usual, but they were definitely hungry. We also learned frogs are actually cannibals, as we watched them attack each other in combat—the winner eating the loser. Now, I know a lot of shit, strange tidbits, weird facts—I'm a great person to have on your Trivial Pursuit team—but I don't know dick about amphibian instincts. I don't know if the frogs were binge-eating each other because they were suddenly as hungry as the snakes and birds, or if they were greedily trying to thin their own herds to enjoy the flies for themselves.

Maybe they knew what we were about to find out. Maybe it wasn't hunger, but suicide.

The number of frogs was quickly reduced and seemed to return to normal. The flies that remained bred. Their numbers increased again.

I hate that buzzing sound.

But nature stepped in to take care of the problem once and for all.

A part of me isn't really surprised where this has gone. Not after seeing it happen right in front of me that last morning at our house. It's only been a little over a month, but seems like a lifetime ago when I witnessed a simple house spider catch one of those flies. I remember smiling about it. Laughing hysterically, actually.

I don't smile anymore.

At least the frogs weren't a threat to us. We may never know if the frogs were infected after they ate the flies. We may never know if they carried the disease with them at all. It didn't matter, so we didn't consider it. They were only around for a couple weeks, and more importantly, frogs don't generally bite humans.

Spiders, however, bite.

Arachnophobia has strange degrees to it. Some people fear them all, others hate just the big ones, and then there are those who have strange prejudices against the brightly colored or albino types. While I've never been afraid of them, I've never really liked them. Now? Now, I fear them all.

Jerry has turned into a hell of a sidekick. We've buried most of the hatchet between us. Jamie wants to be more helpful, but with Sarah gone, we need her to be on the kids 24/7—though we relieve her as much as we can, and even the boys help out with the baby. We survived winter. We made it through the worms and the flies and even the frogs. But I don't know what we're going to do now. Spiders... even the tiniest crack will let those fuckers inside.

The problem is, we don't know which bite and which don't. We don't know if they're infected from eating the flies. We don't know if we've traded one form of death for another. We don't know if they're harmless but voraciously hungry like the birds and snakes had been. And short of finding out the hard way, firsthand, we won't know. So we have to assume the worst.

Spiders come in all shapes and sizes, a rainbow of colors, with different hunting techniques. They're as varied as snowflakes. But they all have one thing in common. Egg sacs have more than a couple babies inside.

I miss the fucking frogs.

~ Nick Kontis, journal entry

Praise for TEETH

Kelli Owen tackles, redesigns, and redefines the hundred-year-old vampire trope

"If you're one of the horror fans who have grown tired of our fanged friends, then Kelli Owen's Teeth puts some serious bite back into an anemic genre."
~ Ink Heist

"Kelli Owen has created her own vampire mythos and in so doing erased nearly everything that has come before."
~ Horrible Book Reviews

"Characterization is one of [Kelli Owen's] greatest strengths as a writer, and she's taken it to a whole new level with Teeth."
~ Gingernuts of Horror

"[Kelli Owen] taps into the fears and emotions of her characters to deliver an entertaining story with depth."
~ This is Horror

"When we hear of 'world-building' in genre fiction most of us automatically think of fantasy and science fiction but Kelli Owen gives the likes of George RR Martin a serious run for their money..."
~ Tony Jones, Ink Heist

TEETH

All myths have a kernel of truth.
The truth is: *vampires are real.*

They've always been here, but only came out of hiding in the last century. They are not what Hollywood would have you believe. They are not what is written in lore or whispered by the superstitious.

They look and act like humans. They live and love and die like humans. Puberty is just a bit more stressful for those with the recessive gene. And while some teenagers worry about high school, others dread their next set of teeth.

Vampires are real, but in a social climate still struggling to accept that truth, do teeth alone make them monsters?

(see following pages for an excerpt...)

— PROLOGUE —

The tall, skinny man sat and flipped his armchair lever in a smooth, practiced motion—the footrest slamming upward to meet his feet. He pushed the button on the remote, and the television came *blaring* to life—the volume unexplainable in the otherwise quiet house. He reached up and gathered his shoulder-length hair into a low pony, expertly hooking the rubber band from his wrist around the loose strands.

A dog barked several houses over—a quick yip to greet a wandering cat, or an awareness of *his* presence. The couple across the street could be heard talking in excited tones through their open windows, whether they were arguing or naturally loud was unclear. The figure blocked out them *and* the dog, along with the distant sounds of sparse traffic on Main Street.

Looking through a gap in the curtains partially covering the window of the back door, he watched the skinny man's actions. The long narrow home made it easy to survey the layout, and was partially why it was chosen. The inside was as desolate and depressing as the neighborhood around it. The walls were bare of portraits, the garbage was full of empty tequila bottles and paper plates, and the table was stacked with job applications and unemployment stubs. He had no family, no friends, no job, no life. He had no business left unfinished.

No one will miss this one.

The man reached into the crumpled McDonald's bag and pulled a Big Mac free. The peace symbol tattooed on his inner wrist was briefly visible and completed the hippie persona the figure had perceived. The man expertly flicked the top of the cardboard container open, as canned laughter from the television faded into a commercial for Andy's Auto, the local car dealership. He lifted the burger's bun and pulled two pickles free, apparently believing it was easier to remove them than to request a special order.

As the television switched over to an obnoxiously loud commercial for *American Idol*, the figure opened the back door. The telltale creak a tenant may recognize was easily overpowered by the bad vocals in the living room.

The figure loved small-town mentality and wondered how long it would be before they began locking their doors, leaving outside lights on, and closing their curtains. Until then, he'd have free reign and he was going to enjoy it. Slipping into the house, he slinked across the cracked kitchen linoleum. The figure snuck up behind the man as he took the first bite from the heat lamp preserved sandwich.

The figure's motions sped up as he approached and he pierced the unsuspecting man's neck before the hippie had time to react. The man's eyes shot wide open as his blood poured from the wound in his jugular. The slickness squirted with an initial burst of pressure, pumped from a still-beating heart, before the fountain waned to a steady flow down the front of a dirty Dave Matthews t-shirt.

The figure quickly collected the spilling blood and watched the dying man with fascination.

Terror held the hippie motionless—his hand still in midair, but his sandwich fallen apart in his lap. His eyes widened as his fingers flicked briefly and moved sporadically, gesturing frantically toward his neck. Before he could wrap his hand around the wound or somehow apply enough pressure to stop the hemorrhaging, he began choking and spitting up flecks of blood.

He gasped and the figure knew whatever blood wasn't coming *out* of the wound was rushing toward the man's lungs. The man sputtered and seized briefly, before the will and fight faded in his eyes—much sooner than expected. Unblinking fear held is eyes open wide as their spark faded, and slowly the shine was replaced with a wordless matte plea. The man's lips were partially open, as if to speak, or robotically chew the bite still in his mouth.

A cruel smile spread across the figure's lips.

Vampires had stepped from the shadows almost fifty years ago and the world at large had renamed them, and welcomed them. Some wanted to *be* them. Others refused to accept them. After three decades of fear and confusion, a treaty was supposed to make everyone complacent neighbors—a new term for them, a clean slate for their history.

But technology gave voice to everyone with an Internet connection and social media caused havoc. Laws were suggested almost daily to *force* tolerance. Libel suits were being filed against historical belief and folklore. Prejudices were alive and well, and as real as the vampires. The *lamians*. The humans were torn between over-eager liberal acceptance and stoic intolerance bred by ignorance and fear. The *vampires* continued to claim they shouldn't be judged as a whole. It was upheaval and protests, banding together in song, and social warriors shaking fists at proclaimed indignities they'd chosen to fight for even though they weren't asked.

The figure found it all disgusting. *All* of it.

Vampires should have remained a secret. The humans should have remained afraid of the dark. And here, in the muddy waters of change, the figure knew he would wallow in their mistakes as he explored the taste of their deaths. He shut his eyes for a moment and inhaled deeply, enjoying the smell of blood as it washed over the room.

The life from victim number three succumbed as the slow trickle came to a stop, and the figure stood. He left the television on and the back door open. Stepping into the cool night air, he felt a chill on his skin where the blood had spattered. He whistled through his teeth, hoping to attract the barking dog. Let the animals feast on the meat he'd left behind. He had what he needed.

He'd taken the blood.

Made in the USA
Lexington, KY
12 November 2019